LARRYBOY
AND THE ABOMINABLE TRASHMAN

www.bigidea.com

Zonder**kidz**™

The children's group of Zondervan
www.zonderkidz.com

Larryboy and the Abominable Trashman
Copyright © 2004 by Big Idea Productions, Inc.

Requests for information should be addressed to:
Zonderkidz, Grand Rapids, Michigan 49530

ISBN: 0-310-70652-1

Written by: Doug Peterson
Editor: Cindy Kenney
Cover and Interior Illustrations: Michael Moore
Cover Design and Art Direction: Paul Conrad, Karen Poth
Interior Design: Holli Leegwater, John Trent, and Karen Poth

CIP applied for
Printed in United States

04 05 06/RRD/5 4 3 2 1

BIG IDEA BOOKS

AND THE ABOMINABLE TRASHMAN

WRITTEN BY
DOUG PETERSON

ILLUSTRATED BY
MICHAEL MOORE

BASED ON THE HIT VIDEO SERIES: LARRYBOY
CREATED BY PHIL VISCHER
SERIES ADAPTED BY TOM BANCROFT

Zonderkidz

TABLE OF CONTENTS

CHAPTER 1

CANNED MONSTER

Junior Asparagus hated taking out the trash at night—especially on a foggy night like this one. Wind whipped through the trees. Leaves spun around on the ground. The swings on the swing set were creaking in the breeze. Every sound made Junior's heart beat faster.

The Asparagus family kept *two* garbage cans out back by the garage, which were buried deep in shadow. At any moment, Junior expected something snarling to leap out at him.

"That's strange," he said, edging closer to the garbage cans. As his eyes slowly adjusted to the darkness, he could see *three* garbage cans. "I thought we had only two cans. Mom and Dad must've bought a new one," he said, as a shiver ran up his spine, did two laps around his neck, and sprinted back down.

Then it happened.

Just as Junior was about to lift the lid on the new can, the container began to move. It shook and rattled as if something was inside trying desperately to get out.

Junior dropped his garbage bag. His mouth opened wide, but he made no sound.

One heart-stopping second later, the silver lid on the new can popped off and shot eight feet into the air. That was something Junior didn't see every day. Inside the can, the garbage swirled around and around, like a whirlpool of gunk, slop, and litter. Faster and faster it spun. Then, with a roar and a **WHOOOOOSH,** the trash came together and rose up out of the can.

The garbage was *alive!*

Even stranger, the trash took on the shape of a creature. It had arms made out of discarded paper-towel tubes and Chinese take-out containers. Its head looked like it was formed out of wrinkled wrappers of all sorts. And the creature's chest was nothing but stale donuts, banana peels, and a half-eaten fish

Even worse—the monster smelled like moldy meat, spoiled milk, and rotten eggs.

"AAAAAAHHHHHHHHHHHH!"

That was Junior screaming, in case you hadn't already guessed.

The creature rose out of the garbage can, swinging his trashy arms wildly and bellowing like a gorilla in bad need of a breath mint. The little asparagus wheeled around and dashed back to the house.

Boy, did Junior hate taking out the trash!

CHAPTER 2

EYE-WITNESS

Meanwhile, at Bob the Tomato's house on the other side of Bumblyburg...

"What story do we have for the front page?" Bob said into his cordless telephone. Bob was the busy editor for the *Daily Bumble* newspaper. And like all busy editors, he was doing two things at once. He was taking out the garbage while talking on the phone.

"What!?" Bob shouted into the receiver as he bounced out the back door of his house.

"*Winklesteen Walks Dog?!* What kind of front-page story is that? If the dog had walked Winklesteen, then you'd have a story. But not *Winklesteen Walks Dog*. It's boring!"

On the other end of the phone was Vicki Cucumber, the photographer for the *Daily Bumble*.

"Sure, Phil Winklesteen was big news last month when he rescued seven puppies from Bumbly Bay," Bob said. "But since then, we've done *twenty* stories about Phil Winklesteen. Yes, I know that Phil is a big movie star. But that doesn't mean we have to report on every little thing he does!"

It was true. Phil Winklesteen *was* a big star in action movies. But Phil became more than just another movie star last month when he jumped into Bumbly Bay to rescue those poor little puppies.

He became a *real* action hero!

"I know...I know," Bob muttered into the phone. "Hey, hold on a second, Vicki."

Bob stared at his garbage cans lined up along the side of his house.

"That's odd," he said. "Somebody put a new garbage can next to my house. Yes, I'm sure it's new. I wonder where it came from."

As Bob moved closer, the garbage can began to shake.

"You aren't going to believe this," he said to Vicki over the phone. "But I think there are raccoons in my trash again."

Carefully, Bob lifted up the lid of the shiny, new can. What he saw was the last thing he ever thought he would see.

On the other end of the line, Vicki heard Bob mumble, "What in the world?" Then she heard him gasp, drop the trash-can lid, and scream.

The line went dead.

CHAPTER 3

TALES FROM THE TRASH CAN

Bumblyburg was buzzing.

The next morning, everyone was talking about the monster that had appeared all over town. The creature had leaped out of garbage cans and scared the living daylights out of everyone—including Bob the Tomato. The good news was that Bob survived his "close encounter of the trashy kind."

At the *Daily Bumble*, Bob called an emergency meeting to talk about the monster. Ten staff members crowded around the long oak table as a team of body-gourds barged through the double doors. These were buff-looking gourds in dark suits and dark sunglasses. They encircled the trash can in the *Daily Bumble* meeting room.

"Target secure," said one of the gourds

through a tiny radio. "I repeat. Target secure."

It wasn't until the gourds gave the all-clear signal that Larry the Janitor entered the meeting room—cautiously.

"I just need to empty this trash can," Larry explained to Bob as his bodygourds X-rayed the can. "With a trash monster on the loose, one can never be too careful around garbage. So don't mind us."

Bob sighed and shook his head. Then he turned to his staff and said, "So what headline do we have for today's paper?"

"What do you think of this?" Junior asked Bob. He held up the front page of the *Daily Bumble*, which said in big, bold type: **MONSTER TRASHES CITY!**

"I love it!" Bob declared, scribbling on the news story with his red pencil. "But throw on a couple more exclamation points. That monster is really scary!"

That day the entire newspaper was devoted to the mysterious monster and the twenty-seven eye-witness accounts.

"We also need a name for the monster," Bob said excitedly. "Something that'll really grab 'em."

"How about the Incredible Trash Thing?" suggested

Vicki. "People like monsters that have the word *thing* in the name."

"I like the Smelly Slop Stomper," said Lois Lemon.

The names came fast and furious.

"How about the Trash Mummy?"

"The Can-Man!"

"Can Kong!"

"The Loch Mess Monster!"

"Not bad," commented Bob.

"Gunzilla!" interjected another.

"Even better."

"How about the Abominable Trashman?"

"Who said that?" Bob shouted, bringing a sudden hush to the table.

"I did," chirped Larry the Janitor, as he sifted through the garbage can. Larry cleared his throat and continued. "You've heard of the Abominable Snowman, right? Well...this guy seems pretty abominable?"

Bob spun around in his swivel chair as he gave it some thought. Then...

"I love it!" Bob shouted, scribbling the name on a sheet of paper and handing it to an assistant. "Good work, Larry.

Now, the next thing we need to do is get a photo of the Abominable Trashman. Of all the twenty-seven places he showed up last night, we don't have a single picture to prove that he exists."

"What you need, Chief, is a stakeout," said Larry, glancing up from the trash can.

"Huh?"

"A stakeout," Larry repeated. "Somebody should watch a trash can all night and be ready with a camera."

"That's not a half-bad idea," Bob said. "Vicki, are you up for a job like that?"

"Sure thing, Chief."

Larry the Janitor stopped what he was doing to stare at Vicki. He had a goofy grin on his face and sighed deeply.

"Hey, I have an idea," Larry said after his brain finally came back to earth. "Why don't I help Vicki with the stakeout?"

"Well, I don't know…You're not a reporter or a photographer."

"But I'm a janitor! And who knows more about garbage cans than a janitor?"

"You've got a point," Bob agreed. "And the stakeout

was your idea in the first place."

So it was settled. Larry the Janitor and Vicki the Cucumber would stand guard by the Asparagus family's garbage cans at nightfall. And Larry would get a chance to spend time with Vicki—which made him quite happy.

Little did Vicki know, however, that Larry the Janitor wasn't who he appeared to be. Mild-mannered Larry was really the caped cucumber...the green guardian of Bumblyburg...the plunger-headed protector of all that is decent and good.

Larry was none other than *Larryboy!*

HE ...IS...THAT...HERO!

CHAPTER 4

MONSTER WATCH

Larry the Janitor and Vicki the Cucumber crouched behind a huge pile of garbage bags filled with leaves. It was pitch-black dark behind the Asparagus house, and the only sounds in the neighborhood were the chirping of crickets, the barking of faraway dogs—and Larry's heartbeat.

Larry was nervous. But it wasn't just the idea of a monster pouncing on him that stirred his fears. Larry was afraid that he wouldn't come up with anything good to talk about with Vicki.

"Uh...Nice night we're having," Larry said, looking around.

"Yes. Nice night," Vicki answered, fumbling for something to say.

Larry smiled awkwardly. "Uh...Did you

know that every person in the country throws away about four pounds of garbage every day?"

"No." Big pause. "I didn't." Vicki looked around. Normally, she was never at a loss for words.

"Are you afraid of the Abominable Trashman?" she finally asked, as she checked to make sure her camera was loaded with film.

"Not a bit," said Larry. "I don't have a scared bone in my body." Larry was afraid to admit that he had *several* scared bones in his body, not to mention a scared heart, scared gallbladder, scared tongue, and scared lips.

Suddenly, the crickets stopped chirping and the dogs stopped barking. A brisk wind sent a stream of leaves rushing along the ground. Branches scraped against each other, looking like skeleton arms. Something strange was happening.

"This could be it," said Larry, peeking over a bag of leaves.

They watched the three garbage cans that were not more than ten feet away. Ever so slightly, the newest of the cans started to move. Then the lid began to shake, rattle, and roll.

"Here he comes!" whispered Larry excitedly. "Are the lights set?"

Vicki nodded. They had set up floodlights and were going to flick them on the moment the monster appeared.

The entire garbage can began to shake, rattle, and rock. Vicki looked into the camera.

Everything went completely and utterly still for one-billionth of a moment. Then...

POP!

The lid shot up into the air like a cork out of a volcano.

WHOOOOOOSHHHHH!

A living mass of moldy rags and putrid potato peels rose up and out of the can, swinging its arms like a blind zombie.

FLASH!

The night lit up with the glare of four floodlights.

CLICK! CLICK! CLICK!

With light flooding the garbage cans, Vicki snapped photo after photo. These were going to be the most amazing pictures of her life!

At first, the Abominable Trashman was stunned by the sudden blast of light. Then he became angry, leaped out of the garbage can, and headed straight for Vicki.

Vicki stumbled backward, tripped over a stone, and landed on her back. But she scrambled right back up and made a run for it. She could smell the breath of the monster as he closed in on her. It smelled like spoiled cabbage, year-old stew, and a plate of moldy anchovies.

Just when Vicki thought she was going to get away, something snagged the strap on her camera. She was yanked backward, like a fish on a hook.

"*HELLLLLPPPP!*" The Abominable Trashman had her in his gloppy clutches.

"Larry! *Help me!*"

Vicki cast a terrified look over her shoulder, expecting to see Larry running to her aid. Instead, he was running in the opposite direction. Larry the Janitor vanished into the trees, leaving Vicki all alone to face the monster.

CHAPTER 5

MONSTER MASH

Vicki's life flashed before her eyes like a movie with coming attractions of heaven. The Abominable Trashman smashed her camera to bits and dragged her back toward the garbage can.

But just at that moment, something zipped from out of the darkness.

THONK!

A plunger came flying from the trees and caught the monster square in the back.

"Prepare to be recycled, banana breath!" Those brave words came from none other than the Veggie defender—Larryboy! The caped cucumber hopped out of the bushes and struck a heroic pose.

Unfortunately, he spent a little too long posing. The monster ripped the plunger from his back and hurled it back at Larryboy like a harpoon. Catching Larryboy right in the kisser, it completely covered his face. What's worse, Larryboy couldn't pull the supersuction plunger off, causing an instant blackout—Larryboy couldn't see anything.

The monster heaved Vicki aside and closed in on our purple hero. Larryboy could smell him coming.

With a daring back flip, Larryboy avoided the monster and fired off his second plunger ear. The heat-seeking plunger zeroed in on the monster with incredible accuracy.

THONK!

The plunger hit the Abominable Trashman squarely in the mug, completely covering his face.

This put the two opponents in an interesting spot. Larryboy still couldn't see. But now the Abominable Trashman couldn't see either. Stranger yet, Larryboy and the Trashman were connected to each other by the cords attached to each plunger.

"Time to take out the trash, man!" Larryboy shouted as he blindly ran into a tree.

"*ROARRRR!*" the Trashman bellowed as he blindly banged into the side of the garage.

"Prepare to be trashed, anchovy arms!" Larryboy

yelled, giving a karate kick to the tree. He followed up with two head butts. "That's a tree!" Vicki shouted. "It's not the Trashman!"

"Boy, am I glad to hear that," Larryboy said, shaking his noggin. "I thought this guy had abs of steel!" Then our purple-headed hero did a triple spin in the air and declared, "Prepare to do the dance of doom, Monster Mash!"

Only one problem. After all of this spinning, Larryboy and the Abominable Trashman got all tangled up in Larryboy's plunger cords. The two were tied up, back-to-back.

"Vicki, where is he now?" Larryboy shouted.

"He's right behind you!"

Still blinded by the plunger, Larryboy spun around to face the monster. But because the Trashman was strapped to Larryboy's back, when our hero spun around, so did the Abominable Trashman.

"Take that, you rotten rascal!" said Larryboy as he lunged forward again, but caught nothing but air.

"Where'd he go, Vicki? Where'd he go?"

"He's right behind you, Larryboy!"

"Boy, this monster is quick!"

Larryboy spun around again.

"Now where is he, Vicki?"

"Behind you!"

"And now?"

"He's still behind you!"

This happened about ten times before Larryboy realized that this strategy might not work.

The monster's smell was stronger than ten skunks with hygiene problems, but Larryboy was prepared. He was wearing his "Ocean-Mist Utility Belt." One push of the button and out popped a can of deodorant, a bar of scented soap, a container of potpourri (ask your mom what that is), and two cans of ... *laser-guided air freshener!*

Larryboy fired double-barreled squirts of air freshener, and the air around the monster melted into scents of lilacs and roses.

It drove the Abominable Trashman absolutely nutty.

Swatting at the cloud of flowery air freshener, the monster roared, coughed, and tore at the cords that bound him. When the cords were finally shredded, the Trashman leaped back inside the garbage can and disappeared into the night.

Everything was quiet once again. Vicki was so happy to be alive that she didn't even care that her camera had been destroyed, along with the photos in it.

"Larryboy! That was the bravest thing I've ever seen anyone do!" she said, her eyes glittering in the floodlight. "That took more courage than Phil Winklesteen jumping into Bumbly Bay to save those seven puppies!"

Larryboy blushed beneath his mask. "Aw, gee Vicki, it was nothing."

"It was much more than nothing! It was Larry the Janitor who did nothing! I'm very disappointed in him. He left me all alone with that monster!"

Vicki's words stung. "But Vicki, don't be so hard on Larry. He did—"

"What? He didn't do *anything* to help me. But *you*—you were incredibly brave!"

Larryboy was speechless. He didn't know what to say. Larryboy was a success. But Larry the Janitor was a failure in Vicki's eyes.

CHAPTER 6

SLAVES TO FEAR

Leaving Larryboy to ponder his predicament, we now go deep below the streets of Bumblyburg.

All kinds of supervillains had built their secret lairs beneath the city, including the onion-headed master criminal of all time, Awful Alvin. Alvin's lair had it all—built-in shark pools, piranha tanks, and a dining-room table with a trapdoor beneath every chair. In fact, Alvin's lair was so amazing that it had even appeared on the cover of the magazine *Better Lairs and Gardens*.

Awful Alvin was in an awfully good mood. He was singing karaoke to the song "B-Burg, B-Burg, What an Abominable Town." He was also dancing around the lair with his partner in crime, Lampy—a sidekick who happened to be…well…a lamp.

"My plan is working flawlessly," Alvin cackled as he tap-danced on top of his coffee table. "I have created the perfect monster, and now everyone in Bumblyburg is too scared to take out the trash! What do you think of that, Lampy?"

Lampy didn't answer. Lamps don't usually have much to say.

"Dance with me, Lampy!" Alvin shouted as he twirled Lampy into the next room, where a television studio had been set up. Hundreds of TV sets filled one huge wall, each of them showing pictures of different garbage cans in town.

"I've struck fear in the lives of the citizens of Bumblyburg! When I make people afraid, I have them in my power!" Alvin explained as he wheeled a television camera into the room for Lampy to see. "And when I have people in my power, they'll do *anything* I tell them to do! They're slaves to their fear! And that makes them slaves to *me!* **HA-HA-HA-HA-HA-HA!**"

Alvin set Lampy in front of the television camera and dabbed some makeup on the lampshade.

"Today, you're going to be a TV star, Lampy!" Alvin shouted with diabolical glee. "I'd like you to announce my evil plan to all of Bumblyburg—on prime-time TV. I've even made some cue cards for you!"

Alvin held up the cards, upon which he had scribbled, in crayon, the words that Lampy was to read. Then Awful Alvin turned on the television camera, counted down from five, and pointed at Lampy.

"You're on, Lampy! Lights! Camera! Villainy!"

CHAPTER 7

AND NOW A WORD FROM OUR BLACKMAILERS...

Meanwhile, Larryboy sipped iced tea as he watched his favorite television show.

"That Jethro just cracks me up," Larryboy said to his butler, Archie, who also happened to be an amazing inventor and high-tech wiz.

"I'm pleased to hear that, Master Larry," said Archie, who sat nearby. "However, I couldn't help but notice that you're not laughing out loud and iced tea isn't shooting out of your nose, like it normally does when you watch that show."

There was a long pause.

"You're right, Archie," Larryboy said, spinning around to face his friend. "I admit it. I'm still bothered by what Vicki said to me last night.

She said she was very disappointed in Larry the Janitor! She thinks I'm afraid!"

"Well, you did say she saw you run into the bushes," Archie observed.

"Then maybe I should tell her that Larry the Janitor and Larryboy are the same person. I'm afraid that if I don't, she'll never talk to Larry the Janitor again!"

Archie quickly turned to face Larryboy. "Tell her your secret identity? I would not advise that, Master Larry."

"But I'm afraid that—"

"You're just going to have to deal with it. You're going to have to—"

Suddenly, Larryboy's show vanished from the TV. In its place, the silent image of a lamp popped onto the screen. But it wasn't just any old lamp.

"Hey look, Archie!" said Larryboy. "It's Lampy! What's he doing on TV?"

"That's most unusual," Archie agreed, pulling up his seat next to Larryboy. "Lampy is usually rather shy."

Larryboy and Archie sat in the darkened cave, watching the image of Lampy. But there was no sound.

"Nothing's happening," Larryboy whispered to Archie.

"Why isn't there any sound?"

At that instant, Awful Alvin appeared on the screen and shouted, "Turn on the closed captioning! The closed captioning!"

"Oh. Right. Closed captioning," Larryboy said, pointing his remote at the television. By pushing the closed-captioning button, the following words could be seen, being scrolled along the bottom of the screen:

People of Bumblyburg, be afraid. Be very afraid. Awful Alvin has created the most fearsome creature to ever appear in a garbage can (even scarier than used tissue)! I speak, of course, of the Abominable Trashman.

The Abominable Trashman will continue to terrify your city unless you become his slaves. And as his slaves, you must do certain things for him...or else!

1. Get rid of all real, rubber, or plush chickens (any pictures of them, too).

2. Throw away all polyester pants.

3. Every night, stand outside the house,

wearing a lampshade on your head while holding a bright light. Anyone who does not obey these rules will receive a visit from the Abominable Trashman! Be afraid. Be very afraid! **HA-HA-HA-HA!**

We now return you to your regularly scheduled program.

Lampy vanished from the screen in a storm of static.

"I don't like the looks of this," said Larryboy. "I really enjoy my polyester leisure suit."

"Those are certainly strange demands," said Archie. "But look here, Master Larry. I think I may have discovered something."

Larryboy looked over Archie's shoulder at the computer screen. "What are those squiggly red lines crisscrossing your map of Bumblyburg?"

"They're underground tunnels," Archie explained. "And the tunnels run to every house in Bumblyburg. If my calculations are correct, I believe the tunnels are connected to the new garbage cans that have been sprouting up all around town."

"You mean...?"

"Yes! That's how the monster is appearing in garbage cans everywhere. The monster crawls through the tunnels and jumps out of the cans!"

"You mean...?"

"Yes! The only way we'll be able to stop the monster is if you drop into one of the trash cans, crawl through the tunnels, and track down the creature!"

"You mean...?"

"Yes! That means you're going to have to conquer your fear of small, enclosed spaces."

Larryboy gulped. He hated tight spaces. In fact, that's one of the main reasons why Larryboy was terrified of using the secret pneumatic Larrytube transporter—a tube that could carry him from the newspaper office to the Larrycave in the blink of an eye.

Larryboy was afraid. He was very afraid.

CHAPTER 8

A SECRET-IDENTITY CRISIS

The next morning, when Larry the Janitor arrived at the *Daily Bumble*, he saw Vicki working at her desk. This was his chance to make things right with her. But Vicki left right away, as if she were trying to avoid him.

Larry didn't track her down until the end of the day, when he found her at the water cooler.

"Vicki, you don't understand what happened tho other night," Larry said, desperately.

"I understand perfectly. You got frightened and left me in the clutches of a monster. What else is there to say?"

"But there's another side of me that's very brave," Larry insisted. "You just don't know it."

Vicki shook her head sadly and sighed.

Then, as she hopped away, she said over her shoulder, "I've got photos to take, Larry. Maybe we can talk later."

There had to be something that Larry could do to prove to Vicki that he wasn't a complete chicken. If only he could tell her that he was Larryboy. If only he could tell her that the reason he ran away was to change into his superhero costume!

It was so tempting....Maybe he could tell her....maybe...just maybe...

He decided to do it.

Before he could change his mind, Larry yanked a piece of paper from Bob's desk and scribbled it all down. In the note, he told Vicki that *he* was Larryboy. *He* was that hero of Bumblyburg! *He* was the one who battled the Abominable Trashman.

Trying not to think about what he was doing, Larry sealed the envelope, stuck the letter on Vicki's desk, and then dashed outside.

Larry felt good about what he had done...for about two minutes. But with every step he took closer to home, a different question popped into his mind.

What if Vicki tells her friends? What if Vicki reveals my

secret in a news story? And what will happen if every villain learns my secret identity?

Suddenly, Larry came to a dead stop. His eyes bugged out. *"What have I done?"*

Wheeling around, Larry tore back to the newspaper. He had to get that letter back! He just had to!

He sprinted up five flights of stairs, burst into the newsroom, knocked over Bob the Tomato, and sent papers flying everywhere. He scrambled to Vicki's cubicle and dove toward her desk. Where was it? *Where was it?*

The letter was gone…and so was Vicki.

His secret was out.

CHAPTER 9

THE SUBSTITUTE MONSTER

That night, Larryboy crept into his weekly
Superhero 101 class at Bumblyburg Community
College—the only class in the world for vegetables
with powers far beyond those of normal Veggies. He
was afraid that his classmates would somehow learn
that he had broken one of the biggest superhero rules:
never give away your secret identity.

So, with worries eating away at him, today's les-
son was quite fitting: "How Superheroes Battle Fear."

Unfortunately, the class professor, the wise and
wonderful Bok Choy, was gone that evening.
When the superheroes arrived, they found a
message scrawled on the blackboard: "Bok
Choy cannot make it tonight. Your
substitute teacher

will be Miss Eville." (It also looked like someone had written and then erased **"HA-HA-HA-HA"**.)

"I don't like the looks of this," Larryboy whispered to Lemon Twist, the superhero girl in the seat next to him. "Where's our substitute?"

There was absolutely no sign of the substitute teacher—just an empty chair at the front of the room.

"I was a substitute teacher once," said the Scarlet Tomato, "at a junior high. Talk about scary. I would never have survived all those spitballs without my superpowers."

"I've never heard of Miss Eville," griped Electro-Melon, a hulking fruit with anger-management problems.

Five minutes passed. Still no sign of the teacher.

"I say we call it a night," suggested Larryboy, gathering up his Superhero Handbook.

But before he could rise from his seat, the classroom door slammed shut and locked—all by itself. Then the windows came sliding down and the lights went out, plunging the room into darkness. There was no escape.

A lot of superhero hearts suddenly began to beat superfast.

"I knew I should have taken Superhero Cape

Crocheting 101 this semester," said Larryboy.

Panic was rising fast. And then the garbage can near the front of the room began to shake, rattle, and roll.

"It's the Abominable Trashman!"

The fear was so thick that you could cut it with a knife. You could even scoop it with a spoon, flip it with a spatula, or pick it up with chopsticks.

"Hold it, you guys!" Larryboy shouted. "We're superheroes! We can't be pushed around by one little garbage monster!"

"Good point."

"Hadn't thought about that."

So the superheroes did what every superhero does in a sticky situation. They used their superpowers. Electro-Melon fired up his electrical field. Lemon Twist unleashed her tornado powers. And Larryboy launched his plunger ears.

"OK class, that's enough. Settle down now," came a calm voice by the door. The lights flicked back on, and there stood Bok Choy.

"Bok Choy! We thought you couldn't make it."

"So sorry," said Bok Choy. "There was never really going to be a substitute teacher. Instead, I was giving you a pop quiz. But first let me thank the Invisible Carrot Twins for their help."

Two invisible carrot superheroes slowly materialized in front of the classroom and bowed. They were the ones who had closed the door and windows and made the garbage can rattle.

"How many of you felt fear just now?" asked Bok Choy.

At first, no one answered.

"It's OK to admit it."

"Well...I guess I did say that I wished I had taken Superhero Cape Crocheting," Larryboy admitted, a little embarrassed.

"It's OK to feel fear," Bok Choy said. "Being brave doesn't mean that you never feel fearful. When you're faced by a villain with the power to squash you flat, who wouldn't be afraid?" Bok Choy went on to explain that what makes people brave is how they respond to fear. Do they let fear control them? Do they make wrong decisions when they're afraid? Or do they continue to do the right thing, even when they're scared?

Bok Choy asked the class to open their Superhero Handbooks to Section 19, Paragraph 34, Line 4. The handbook said: "I looked to the LORD, and he answered me. He saved me from everything I was afraid of."

"God will give you brave hearts, even when you're scared silly," said Bok Choy, walking over to the windows. "Look! The people of Bumblyburg have been scared into extreme silliness."

Through the windows, the entire class could see Bumblyburg citizens dumping garbage into their yards because they were too afraid to take it to their trash cans. They could also see people standing outside of their houses with lampshades on their heads while holding bright lights—just as Awful Alvin had ordered.

Like obedient slaves, people did everything Alvin told them to do. They frantically tore pictures of chickens out of their cookbooks and threw them out with the garbage, along with every piece of polyester clothing. Anyone who didn't obey was paid a visit by the Abominable Trashman.

"Fear is taking over the city," said Bok Choy. "It must be stopped."

CHAPTER 10

ROCKET-BOY

"Are you sure this thing is going to work?" Larryboy asked Archie the next day.

"Well...I haven't ironed out all of the kinks in the Larrysled," said Archie. "But we have no choice but to act now."

"Kinks? I don't like the sound of kinks."

The Larrysled was a slick, purple sled with super-suction wheels—perfect for rolling through tunnels at incredibly high speeds. A large rocket was attached to each side.

"If Bob were doing this, we'd call it a Bobsled," Archie joked. But Larryboy was too nervous to laugh.

Archie had also created what looked like an astronaut's space helmet for Larryboy. A little, green, tree-shaped air freshener dangled inside the plastic helmet (important for anyone submerged in week-old glop).

Larryboy waddled over to the garbage can behind the Larrycave—a portal into Awful Alvin's network of tunnels. Then he pushed the orange button on his sled, and the two rockets fired up.

"Well...I guess this is it, Archie old friend," he said, staring into the open garbage can. Larryboy felt like he was about to dive into the intestines of a giant worm. "Tight spaces," he said, woozy with fear. "Why do these tunnels have to be such tight spaces?"

"Remember, Larryboy, God will give you a brave heart to do what's right, even when you're scared silly."

With the flaming Larrysled in his clutches, Larryboy and the rocket-sled teetered on the edge of the garbage can— like someone too afraid to jump off of the diving board. "Are you sure that Lemon Twist isn't interested in this job?"

"You can do it, Master Larry," said Archie, running down the to-do list on his clipboard. Unfortunately, as Archie looked down at his clipboard, he wasn't watching where he was going. He bumped smack into the back of the Larrysled.

BOINKK!

"AHHHHHHHHHHHHHHHH!"

That was Larryboy screaming, in case you hadn't already guessed.

The caped cucumber was knocked forward, fell belly-down on his Larrysled, and tumbled into the bottomless can of disgusting yuck, moldering muck, and decaying gluck.

"Oops," said Archie, staring into the hole at the bottom of the garbage can. "My bad."

Riding the Larrysled, Larryboy roared through a tunnel of rubbish and rot. With blinding speed, he tore through piles of broken toys, decaying food, plastic wrappers, and half-eaten candy bars.

"Are you all right, Larryboy?" came Archie's voice over a radio built into the helmet.

"I'm OK, Archie. But things are pretty gross down here!"

Larryboy zipped like a purple bullet through the tunnels beneath Bumblyburg. Around and around and around and around he raced, as if he were on a never-ending roller-coaster ride. Some of the tunnels were packed with garbage, which smacked against Larryboy's plastic helmet like bugs on a windshield. But other tunnels were clear

sailing and completely free of trash.

"Archie! How do I steer this thing?"

"Use the joystick!" Archie yelled.

"But I'm feeling no joy!" Larryboy yelled, pushing the stick to the right. The Larrysled made a screaming right turn down a new tunnel.

"New problem, Archie."

"What's that, Master Larry?"

"This tunnel has a dead end—emphasis on the word *dead*. How do I stop this thing?"

There was silence for what seemed like forever. "OK, now I remember what that kink in the sled is."

"You mean I can't stop?"

"No, but you can eject. Push the yellow button."

Larryboy pushed the yellow button and out popped a

steaming cup of hot cocoa, served by a robotic arm.

"Sorry," Archie said. "I had that installed for the Larrysled that used to be a snow sled. It was really nice on cold days."

"*Archie!*"

Not far ahead was a solid wall of dirt where the tunnel ended.

"Try the mauve-colored button."

"What color is mauve?" Larryboy asked, frantically pushing every button in sight. The red button controlled the CD player. The blue button served snow cones. The wall was only seconds away.

Larryboy was about to find out what it's like to be a crash-test dummy.

Finally, he jammed down the mauve-colored button, but by then it was too late. The Larrysled hit the wall with such speed that not even a cartoon character could have survived such a crash.

Not even Larryboy.

CHAPTER 11

HEAPS OF TROUBLE

It was a good thing the dirt wall was just a hologram—a 3-D illusion. It wasn't really there.

Larryboy ejected from the Larrysled as it soared through the hologram wall and entered an underground room of some sort. The caped cucumber landed in a huge heap of garbage, while the rocket-sled bored through another mound of trash, hit a real wall...and exploded.

"*Larryboy! Are you OK?*" shouted a frantic Archie over the radio.

"Just fine, Archie. But I'm afraid your Larrysled has seen its last slope. Where am I?"

Larryboy glanced around, knowing that Archie could see through the camera mounted on his helmet.

It was an enormous,

brightly lit room, filled with many mounds of moldering garbage. Millions of flies danced around the trash. (They were doing the jitterbug.) It was a good thing that Larryboy's helmet hadn't cracked, because the smell in the room was enough to stun a full-grown yak with sinus problems.

"My computer shows that the room is connected to Awful Alvin's lair," said Archie. "This must be where Alvin stores the garbage that he stuffs into his tunnels."

"Why does he even bother stuffing his tunnels with trash?"

"To keep people out. You'd have to be incredibly foolish to enter tunnels packed with foul garbage."

"Gee thanks, Archie."

"You know what I mean."

Larryboy scanned the huge room. "I don't see the Abominable Trashman down here," said Larryboy. "So what do I do now?"

Before Archie could answer, all of the lights in the room suddenly went off, plunging Larryboy into darkness.

"What happened, Larryboy? Have I lost the video feed?"

"No. But I've lost all light. I don't like this, Archie. It's downright creepy."

"Use the flashlight mounted on top of your helmet. And remember what Bok Choy told you. It's OK to be afraid. Just don't be a slave to your fear. Keep your head."

"I plan to. It's the only one I've got."

Larryboy clicked on the flashlight and continued to explore with his meager beam of brightness. In the dark, every sound became sharper.

The dripping of water.

The buzz of flies.

The soft steps of someone approaching.

Someone approaching?

Larryboy's heart leaped, and then the alarm built into Larryboy's helmet suddenly started blaring—like a car alarm, but even more annoying.

Trouble was coming.

CHAPTER 12

THERE'S NOTHING TO FEAR BUT FEAR ITSELF (BUT I CAN THINK OF A FEW OTHER THINGS)

Trouble arrived.

Larryboy spun around with cat-like reflexes, fired both of his plungers, knocked the trash monster on his back, tied him up with a sturdy rope, and dragged him to Officer Olaf's paddy wagon.

Well...not quite. That was the way Larryboy imagined it would go.

The real event was a bit tougher.

In truth, the Abominable Trashman pounced on Larryboy from behind, wrapping his slimy arms around him. Larryboy tried to fire both of his plungers. But there was one slight problem. You can't fire supersuction ears when your head is completely covered by a clear, plastic helmet. The suction cups hit the sides of the plastic helmet and attached themselves.

"Sorry, Larryboy," said Archie over the radio. "Finding a way for you to fire your supersuction ears while wearing the helmet was on my to-do list."

"OUCH."

Then the Trashman yanked Larryboy's helmet off, destroying his radio connection to Archie and causing his supersuction ears to retract with a **THOP!** Then he dragged our hero down a long hallway, swung open a heavy, steel door, and hurled Larryboy into a cold and moldy prison cell. The door slammed shut with a **CLANG** that echoed down the hallway.

"Boy, are you a sight for sore eyes," came a voice that startled Larryboy. He wasn't expecting a familiar voice this deep underground.

Larryboy looked up from the floor and blinked twice to make sure he wasn't seeing things.

"Hello, Larryboy," said Vicki Cucumber.

CHAPTER 13

A TRASH-COMPACTION, ACTION HERO

"Vicki! What are you doing here?"

"Just trying to take some photographs," Vicki said. "After my last camera was destroyed, I tried to get new photos of the Abominable Trashman. But that guy really doesn't like having his picture taken."

"I guess I wouldn't want my picture taken if I had stale pizza crusts for a face," said Larryboy, trying to stop his eyeballs from rolling around in their sockets.

"Anyway, the creature caught me and dragged me down here. And I've lost another company camera. Bob's not going to be happy."

Vicki nodded toward the corner, where her smashed camera lay in a big pile of trash.

But what caught Larryboy's eye

was Vicki's camera bag. A letter stuck out of the side pocket. It was Larry's letter! The letter in which he revealed his secret identity!

Larryboy couldn't tell if the letter had been opened or not.

"So how's the weather?" Larryboy said, trying to make small talk as he sidled over toward the camera bag to get a closer look.

"Say cheese, Larryboy!"

A flash went off, catching Larryboy just as he was bending down for a closer look at the envelope. Startled, Larryboy bolted back upright.

"What was *that?*"

"My other camera. Fortunately, I had a spare, mini-camera hidden in my pocket," said Vicki, beaming.

Larryboy smiled weakly. Suddenly, loud voices could be heard from just outside the prison cell. It sounded like people were arguing.

"This could be important," Larryboy said. "Good thing Archie built a listening device into my supersuction ears."

Larryboy fired one of his ears against the cell wall with a THONK and began to listen.

"I can't do it," he heard someone saying. It sounded like the Trashman.

"You have no choice. You're my slave!" said another voice. This one Larryboy recognized.

"It's Awful Alvin," Larryboy whispered to Vicki. "Quick, listen in on my other ear."

Vicki pulled out Larryboy's other supersuction ear and listened through it like it was an old-fashioned telephone.

"But I don't want to hurt the poor cucumber lady or the purple plunger boy," said the Abominable Trashman.

"Why? Larryboy attacked you with air freshener, which you're awfully allergic to!" Alvin said.

"He was just protecting the cucumber lady."

"Do you want me to tell the world your secret?" snarled Awful Alvin.

"*No!* Anything but that!"

"I thought as much," Alvin cackled. (Every villain has to get in his minimum daily allowance of cackling.) "Your fans wouldn't be too happy if they heard that those seven puppies saved *you* from Bumbly Bay—not the other way around!"

"Please don't tell anybody! Please!" begged the

Abominable Trashman.

"I can see the headline now: 'Phil Winklesteen Saved by Puppies!' Your movie career would be over."

"That's what I'm afraid of," whimpered the Trashman.

Could it be true? Was the Abominable Trashman really Phil Winklesteen, the famous action-movie hero from Toledo, Ohio?

"This is amazing," Vicki whispered to Larryboy. "Winklesteen is a celery. So if he's the Trashman, he must be wearing a monster suit of some sort. And his monster arms must be mechanical."

"Ssshhh, they're talking again," said Larryboy.

"Admit it, Winklesteen. You're a slave to your fear," snarled Awful Alvin. "So obey me, and do your job."

"Yes, Master."

Larryboy and Vicki heard what sounded like a heavy lever being yanked. But here's the awful part. The walls of the prison cell began to shake. The gears of a machine groaned from under the floor. And then the walls of the room began to move.

They began to move *inward.*

"Now I know what this room reminds me of," said Vicki.

"It's a giant trash compactor!"

They were about to be smashed like peanut butter and jelly between two giant slabs of concrete bread.

CHAPTER 14

PANIC ROOM

"HA-HA-HA-HA-HA!" cackled Awful Alvin. "When you're gone, Larryboy, no one will be able to stop me from turning every person in this city into my slave!"

Larryboy stuck his face up to a tiny opening in the door to the room—an opening as narrow as a mail slot. "Lampy, you can't let Alvin do this to us!" he shouted to Alvin's sidekick.

"Don't listen to him, Lampy," said Alvin. "It's time we put an end to this purple-headed pest. Come on, Lampy! Let's get out of here!"

"Uh...Larryboy...," said Vicki.

"Lampy, if you turn off this giant trash compactor, I'll buy you a twenty-foot extension cord."

"Uh...Larryboy... "

"Come on, Lampy! Don't let Alvin—"

"*Larryboy!*" Vicki shouted.

"What is it?" Larryboy asked, turning away from the opening in the door.

"You're talking to a lamp."

Larryboy stopped to think for a moment. "Oh. Right. I suppose that's not the wisest use of my time."

"That's what I was thinking, Larry," Vicki said.

"*Larry?* Did you just call me *Larry?*"

Vicki looked shocked. "I mean Larryboy! We've got to find a way out of here, Larryboy!"

Larryboy paused. She knew!

But Larryboy couldn't think about that now. Alvin and Lampy had disappeared down a hallway, leaving Phil Winklesteen (the Trashman) to stand guard.

The caped cucumber struck a dramatic pose. "Have no fear, Vicki, my dear."

Larryboy dug through the mound of trash in the room, pulled a bamboo fishing pole out of the pile, and propped it between the two moving walls.

SNAP!

The fishing pole broke like a giant toothpick.

The walls were now only about ten feet apart and closing in.

"You've got to help us, Mr. Winklesteen!" Vicki yelled through the tiny slit in the door. "You can't just let us be squashed flat like pancakes!"

Vicki could hear Phil Winklesteen moving around just outside the door, but he didn't answer.

"OK, so maybe you didn't save those puppies from Bumbly Bay," shouted Vicki. "But don't be a slave to your fear! God will give you a brave heart to do what's right, even when you're scared silly! This is your chance to show some real courage!"

No answer.

The concrete walls were now about eight feet apart. The gears underneath the floor groaned like mechanical monsters.

Larryboy pulled a discarded surfboard out of the trash and propped it between the walls.

CRACK!

The surfboard snapped into five pieces.

"Phil, if you're afraid to rescue us, that's OK!" Larryboy shouted. "Even superheroes like me are afraid some-times—actually, right now comes to mind. But God can help us to be brave, even when we're scared silly!"

No answer.

The concrete walls were now about six feet apart, inching forward like deadly, concrete glaciers.

Larryboy tried to jam an inflatable rubber raft between the walls.

POP!

"Where's a steel pole when you need one?" Larryboy griped, digging through the trash.

"You've got to help us, Phil!" Vicki yelled.

In desperation, Larryboy shouted the words that he remembered from Bok Choy: "I looked to the Lord, and he answered me! He saved me from everything I was afraid of!"

Inspired by those words, Larryboy did the only thing left to do. He propped himself between the two walls. With the bottom of his cucumber body against one wall and his purple, plunger-eared head against the other wall, our hero gritted his teeth. Vicki marveled at his courage.

She also took a few snapshots.

"Can you make double prints for me?" Larryboy asked. "I'd love a copy for my wallet."

The squeeze was on.

CHAPTER 15

UNMASKING A MONSTER

"I'm doing it!" Larryboy declared in triumph. "It's actually working!"

With Larryboy's body propped in between them, the walls had suddenly stopped moving inward. Amazing!

"Uh…Larryboy…" said Vicki.

"This is incredible!"

"Uh…Larryboy…"

"I have greater powers than I imagined!"

"Uh…Larryboy…Look over here," said Vicki.

Larryboy glanced sideways. The door to the trash-compactor room was wide open. Standing in the doorway was Phil Winklesteen, with his Trashman mask removed.

"Phil turned off the trash compactor," Vicki pointed out. "He's rescuing us."

Larryboy smiled. "I knew that."

"Is it too late to be courageous?" Phil asked.

"It's never too late!" Larryboy shouted, dropping to the ground and striking a dramatic pose.

"Then let's get going!" Phil beamed.

They dashed out of the room and hurried through a secret exit.

"This is great!" Larryboy said. "Once people see that the Abominable Trashman is really Phil Winklesteen, a celery from Toledo, they won't be slaves to their fears anymore. Awful Alvin will no longer control them."

It all seemed too easy.

The three heroes clambered up a metal ladder. Then Phil shoved open a hatch in the roof, which led back above ground. Larryboy bounded through the hatch and struck a dramatic pose, his cape flapping in the breeze.

One second later, his heart sank, and his cape stopped flapping. What Larryboy saw terrified him to the core.

Standing tall over Bumblyburg was another trash monster. Only this monster was a zillion times larger than Phil Winklesteen. This creature was as tall as a five-story building.

It was tall enough to destroy an entire city.

CHAPTER 16

GUNKZILLA

The new monster was a super-sized version of the Abominable Trashman—but much bigger and much more dangerous. *Gunkzilla* was a more fitting name for this monstrous creature.

As Gunkzilla stomped through downtown Bumblyburg, walls crumbled. The earth shook. Veggies fled in all directions. Fear had completely taken over the city.

Correction. Awful Alvin had completely taken over Bumblyburg.

"Winklesteen, did you think you were going to be my one and only monster?" came an evil voice from right behind our heroes. Larryboy, Vicki, and Phil spun around to see Awful Alvin (and Lampy) just yards away in their hovercraft.

"How…how did you do this?" Phil asked.

"I'm glad you asked," Alvin said, eager to brag. "You see, I used you, Phil. I used you to strike fear in the citizens of Bumblyburg. And then I used that fear to power my greatest invention ever—the Trash Reenergizer."

"And what in the world is that?" scowled Vicki.

"The Trash Reenergizer can make garbage come alive and take any shape I want," Alvin cackled. "And it's powered by fear. My machine sucks up people's fear and uses that power to create monsters out of trash. The result is even more fear. You might say it recycles fear. It's very energy efficient."

"A machine that makes trash monsters? This I have to see," said Larryboy. "Where do you keep it?"

"Do you think I'd be ridiculous enough to tell you where I

keep my secret weapon?"

"Why, yes," said Larryboy. "You just told us your entire evil plot."

"Explaining evil plots is required of all villains near the end of stories," Alvin explained. "But the Association of Supervillains does not require us to tell the location of our secret weapons. That's for you to find out." Awful Alvin cackled for what had to have been the fiftieth time that day. (He was close to setting the world record for cackling.) "*Be afraid, Larryboy! Be very afraid!*" Awful Alvin shouted. Then he and Lampy took off in their hovercraft and blazed across the afternoon sky.

"This is all my fault," Phil groaned. "I stirred up fear in Bumblyburg. Now that fear is being used to power Alvin's awful machine. And that machine is being used to create giant trash monsters."

"I just wish we knew what Awful Alvin was afraid of," said Larryboy. "That would come in handy."

Phil blinked in surprise. "You mean you don't know?"

"Well … no. Do you?"

"I thought everybody knew," Phil said. "Awful Alvin has 'alektorophobia,' which is the fear of chickens, and 'noctiphobia,' the fear of darkness. He even has 'textophobia,' which is the fear of fabrics—in his case, polyester."

"So that's why he's been forcing people to rid the city of chickens and polyester pants!" Vicki exclaimed. "And that's why he's been forcing people to wear lampshades and stand around at night with bright lights!"

"Absolutely. He's trying to rid Bumblyburg of everything *he's* afraid of."

"This changes everything," Larryboy said, a gleam coming to his eyes. "Here's what I want you guys to do." Quickly, Larryboy told Phil and Vicki his cunning idea and then added, "I've got to find Archie. It's time to take out some trash!"

CHAPTER 17

BRAVE HEARTS

When Larryboy reached the Larrycave, he found that Archie already had the Larryplane ready to fly. Larryboy leaped into the cockpit and raced toward the heart of Bumblyburg

Finding his first target was easy. He simply had to look for a living pile of garbage five stories high. Gunkzilla had just stepped on a parked car and was trying to shake it loose from the bottom of his foot.

The Larryplane swooped right by the head of the trashy monster, like a pesky fly. The creature tried to swat the plane, but he wasn't quick enough. Larryboy brought the plane around for a second pass and fired four plungers, two from each wing.

The four plungers were magnetized, so they zipped straight for the metal belly of Gunkzilla.

THONK! THONK! THONK! THONK!

"ROWRRRR!" (That's monster for "Oooo, that tickles!")

With the plungers connected to the belly of the beast, Larryboy circled Gunkzilla. Once. Twice. Three times. Every time he circled the monster, the tether lines attached to the plungers wrapped around the large arms of Gunkzilla, tying him up like a bundle of...well...trash.

The monster couldn't budge.

"That'll hold him for a little while. Now it's time to pay a visit to Awful Alvin," Larryboy told Archie over his radio.

"My radar has tracked Alvin's movements," Archie said over the communicator. "He's hiding in the Bumbly Mountains, fourth cave from the left."

Larryboy knew the exact cave. The Not Welcome mat in front of the cave was a dead giveaway.

"So *this* is the Trash Reenergizer," said Larryboy, stepping into the brightly lit cave where Alvin was hiding. In one corner was a huge machine, which looked like it had been built out of junk from the local garbage dump. On top of the contraption was a giant satellite dish, which

soaked up fear and powered the machine. (It also brought
in five hundred television stations, including the All–Fish-
Slapping Network.)

Awful Alvin whirled around. "Rats! What are you doing
here, Larryboy?"

"I'm shutting you down, Awful Alvin."

"That's what you think." An evil gleam glittered in his
oniony eyes. Alvin turned to his trusty sidekick and said,

"There's one thing this superhero didn't plan on, isn't there, Lampy?"

"And what's that?" asked Larryboy.

"*This!*"

Awful Alvin pulled a huge switch on the wall. A garbage can, hanging upside down above Larryboy's head, suddenly dropped from the ceiling before our hero could even react. The can slammed down over Larryboy, trapping him inside.

"You've seen how my Trash Reenergizer can turn ordinary garbage into living monsters," Awful Alvin said with a twisted grin. "What you didn't know is that I can reverse the process. I can also turn living things...into trash!"

With a diabolical laugh, Alvin yanked another humongous lever. Sparks showered down from the ceiling. Bolts of electricity danced alongside the garbage can. Smoke filled the cave.

Then Awful Alvin slowly raised the garbage can.

Larryboy was gone. In his place was a tiny mound of bubblegum wrappers, apple cores, and burned popcorn. Trash. That was all that was left of Larryboy.

CHAPTER 18

CHICKEN!

"AHHHHHHHHHHH!"

Vicki screamed.

She and Phil Winklesteen ran into the cave at the exact moment that Awful Alvin changed Larryboy into a pile of trash. Vicki couldn't believe her eyes.

"AHHHHHHHHHHHH!" That was Awful Alvin's scream. (If you put your ear close to the page, you can tell the difference.)

Why was Alvin screaming? Well, because Phil and Vicki had collected a dozen chickens. And those chickens were standing in the mouth of the cave like gunslingers at a showdown in an old-time Western.

"BWAKKK! BWAKKK! BWAKKK!" (Those were the chickens clucking, in case you hadn't already guessed.)

Awful Alvin had been terrified of chick-

ens ever since he was five years old, when a chicken mistook his oniony head for an egg. The chicken sat on his head for two days, and he hasn't been the same since.

"AHHHHHHHHHH!" Awful Alvin screamed a second time.

"AHHHHHHHHHH!" So did Vicki.

Then total chaos ensued. Awful Alvin picked up Lampy and sprinted out of the cave, screaming like a maniac. The chickens, sensing his fear, went after him like something out of the classic movie, *Attack from Planet Chicken!*

Unfortunately, as Alvin fled from the cave, he dashed right across the pile of trash that had once been Larryboy. He kicked pieces of Larryboy in all directions.

"AHHHHHHHHH!" Phil screamed, running for a broom and dustpan. He wanted to sweep up all of the pieces of Larryboy before they got mixed up with other trash.

Meanwhile, as Alvin dashed out of the cave with

Lampy, followed by the chickens, he grabbed Vicki and took her prisoner. But Phil never noticed any of this because he was too busy sweeping up Larryboy.

"Larryboy! Speak to me!" Phil said to the trash.

"Hi, Phil. Thanks for bringing the chickens. It worked like a charm."

It was Larryboy's voice. Phil couldn't believe it. He looked closely at the pile of trash that he had just swept up. What he didn't see was Larryboy climbing out of the garbage can hanging upside down behind him.

"You can talk?" asked a shocked Phil, thinking that the little pieces of trash could speak.

"Of course I can talk. What were you expecting?"

"Don't worry, Larryboy! We'll figure out a way to put you back together."

Phil held the trash close to his face to see if he recognized Larryboy somewhere in the garbage.

"Nice garbage," Larryboy observed, looking over Phil's shoulder.

"These are pieces of Larryboy," Phil moaned, casting a glance over his shoulder. Then he did a double take.

"AHHHHHHHHH!" That was Phil screaming, in case you

hadn't already guessed.

"But how…?" Phil asked. "We saw—you were changed into trash!"

"Aw, that," said Larryboy. "Alvin's machine never changed me into garbage. His machine is powered by fear, but it didn't work on me, because I wouldn't let fear control me. Instead, I used my supersuction ears to hang onto the inside of the garbage can. When Alvin lifted the can back up, I was lifted up with it.

"I scraped some trash from the bottom of the can onto the ground—to confuse him," our hero added. "That's why he thought it was me. Pretty nifty, eh?" Larryboy glanced around. "Where's Vicki?"

Phil and Larryboy did a quick check of the room. Then they ran out of the cave and looked down the hill.

"**AHHHHHHHHH!**" This time, both Phil and Larryboy screamed at the same time. They could see, far down the hill, Alvin running away with Vicki as his prisoner, Lampy in tow.

"We've got to save her!" Phil shouted.

"I've got an idea," Larryboy said. "Would you grab that garbage can?"

"Sure thing!"

While Phil went to get the garbage can, Larryboy vanished into the bushes. Within seconds, he reemerged as Larry the Janitor.

"What happened to Larryboy?" asked a very confused Phil Winklesteen, when he came back with the garbage can.

"Larryboy asked me to take care of this personally," said Larry. "Have no fear." Then the brave janitor turned the can on its side and climbed into it. "Give me a little push, would you, Phil?"

Phil gave Larry a shove, and the silver garbage can went rolling and bouncing down the slope. Awful Alvin saw the garbage can coming, but he never stood a chance. The can hit a rock, bounced high into the air ... and barreled into Awful Alvin, like a bowling ball hitting a pin. Alvin went flying one direction and Lampy the other.

Phil came running down the slope, rope in hand. "Thought you might need this to tie up the loose ends," he said, handing the rope to Larry.

Before Alvin could regain his senses, Larry had the awful onion and his sidekick tied up like a sack of potatoes and sitting in the garbage can—ready for pickup by Officer Olaf.

CHAPTER 19

A NEW POWER

But the danger wasn't over yet.

Back in the heart of Bumblyburg, Gunkzilla broke loose from the cords that Larryboy had wrapped him in. The monster looked around for something to smash. His eyes (made out of cracked car headlights) locked onto the Burger Bell restaurant. Gunkzilla stomped in its direction, roaring every step of the way.

But that's when the monster began to slow down. Even his roar began to sound like a recording being played in slow motion. Gunkzilla was losing power.

The courage that Larryboy had shown back at the cave was having an effect on the Trash Reenergizer. As the machine sucked up Larryboy's courage, it began to sizzle, steam, rattle, and shake.

Other Veggies who had heard about the heroics also began to gain courage. Soon, bravery spread through Bumblyburg like a fresh wind. As the Trash Reenergizer sucked up this courage, it began to spark. Nuts and bolts holding the contraption together began to wiggle and pop out. The machine was having a complete breakdown. And then...

KABOOM!

The Trash Reenergizer went up in a fire-filled cloud of smoke.

But surprisingly, Gunkzilla didn't stop altogether. His eyes clicked on. His gears shifted. A new surge of energy moved through his trashy body. Gunkzilla was on the move again.

But there was a difference. Free from the power of the Trash Reenergizer, the monster began to clean up the mess he had made.

"Well, I'll be," said Officer Olaf with a big grin on his face. "The trash monster has become a giant garbage collector."

It was true. Gunkzilla tiptoed through the town, picking

up garbage and carrying it to the landfill. Bumblyburg was saved...and getting cleaner by the minute.

CHAPTER 20

SUPER JANITOR

As Bumblyburg returned to normal, Phil Winklesteen did one of the bravest things of his life. He told the people that he hadn't really saved those seven puppies from Bumbly Bay. He admitted that they had saved him.

To his surprise, the thing that he had feared most did not come to pass. The people of Bumblyburg didn't really care that he had been rescued by puppies. Instead, they were amazed by his and Larry the Janitor's courage in helping Larryboy defeat Alvin and Lampy. There was even some talk that his adventure would be made into a book.

As for Larry the Janitor and Vicki Cucumber...

"Larry, I couldn't believe how brave you were," Vicki said, as they headed back toward Bumblyburg. Then she stopped and looked down at the ground. "I'm sorry I got so angry with you the other day. I didn't know..."

"That's OK," Larry smiled.

"But I should've realized how brave you are, Larry. You were fearless!"

"Actually, I wasn't fearless," Larry said, as they continued on. "I was very scared. But Larryboy taught me that God wants us to do brave things even when we're scared silly."

Larry eyed Vicki's camera bag, which still had his letter sticking out of one of the pockets. "Uh…Vicki, did you ever read that letter from me?"

Vicki glanced down at the letter and blushed. "Oh…well, I'm afraid I didn't."

Larry breathed a big sigh of relief.

"I was so upset with you that I never even looked at it," she admitted. "But I'll read it right now."

"No, no, no, that's OK," said Larry, plucking the letter from her bag. "I said some things that I probably shouldn't have."

"I understand."

So Larry ripped up the letter and dropped it into the nearest trash can. Five minutes later, garbage men drove up in their truck, emptied the trash into the hopper, and rode off to the dump. The ripped-up letter wound up forty feet underground in the Bumblyburg Landfill.

Larryboy's secret was buried deep—where it belonged.

As for Awful Alvin...

He and Lampy were arrested on charges of "Assault with a Soggy Banana Peel." Then they were tossed into the Bumblyburg Pig-penitentiary, a prison for trashy criminals. Alvin spent long days plotting a way to escape and get his revenge on Larryboy.

When it was late at night and the darkness made him afraid, Alvin used his sidekick to light up his cell. Lampy was his own personal nightlight.

"We shall return," Alvin vowed, tucking himself into bed. "Good night, Lampy."

Alvin closed his eyes and began to count mutant sheep. "I'll get you, Larryboy," he muttered sleepily. "I'm not afraid of you...I'm not afraid..."

Suddenly, Lampy's lightbulb burned out and Alvin's cell became pitch dark.

"AHHHHHHHHHHHHHHHHHHHHHHHH!"

That was Awful Alvin, in case you hadn't already guessed.

THE END

OWN
COLLECTI
BOOKS AND VIDEOS!

Larryboy and the Amazing Brain-Twister
Softcover 0-310-70651-3

Larryboy in the Good, the Bad, and the Eggly
VHS

BOOKS

Larryboy and the Emperor of Envy (Book 1)
Softcover 0-310-70467-7

Larryboy and the Awful Ear Wacks Attacks (Book 2)
Softcover 0-310-70468-5

Larryboy and the Sinister Snow Day (Book 3)
Softcover 0-310-70561-4

Larryboy and the Yodelnapper (Book 4)
Softcover 0-310-70562-2

Larryboy in the Good, the Bad, and the Eggly (Book 5)
Softcover 0-310-70650-5

Larryboy
Softcover

VIDEOS

Larryboy and the Angry Eyebrows (Episode 1)
VHS

Larryboy in ... Leggo My Ego (Episode 2)
VHS

Larryboy in ... The Yodelnapper (Episode 3)
VHS